Little Skill Seekers

SIGHT WORDS

■SCHOLASTIC

New York • Toronto • London • Auckland • Sydney • New Delhi
Mexico City • Hong Kong • Buenos Aires

Cover Design: Tannaz Fassihi
Cover Illustration: Michael Robertson
Interior Design: Mina Chen
Interior Illustration: Doug Jones

Scholastic Inc., 557 Broadway, New York, NY 10012
ISBN: 978-1-338-30638-5
Copyright © Scholastic Inc. All rights reserved. Printed in the U.S.A.
First printing, March 2019.

3 4 5 6 7 8 9 10   40   24 23 22 21

Dear Parent,

Welcome to *Little Skill Seekers: Sight Words*! The ability to recognize sight words helps to strengthen reading fluency and lays the foundation for reading success—this workbook will help your child develop these skills.

Help your little skill seeker build a strong foundation for learning by choosing more books in the Little Skill Seekers series. The exciting and colorful workbooks in the series are designed to set your child on the path to success. Each book targets essential skills important to your child's development.

Here are some key features of *Little Skill Seekers: Sight Words* and the other workbooks in this series:

- Filled with colorful illustrations that make learning fun and playful

- Provides plenty of opportunity to practice essential skills

- Builds independence as children work through the pages on their own, at their own pace

- Comes in a perfect size that fits easily in a backpack for practice on the go

Now let's get started on this journey to help your child become a successful, lifelong learner!

—The Editors

Trace it.

a   a   a

Write it.

Write a on each shell.

Trace it.

I   I   I

Write it.

Color each apple that has I.

Trace it.

is   is   is

Write it.

Trace it.

to   to   to

Write it.

Circle each frame that has is.

 it

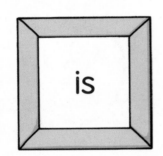 is

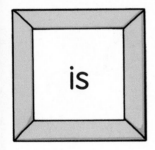 is

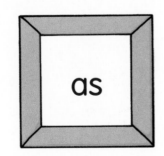 as

Color each space that has to.

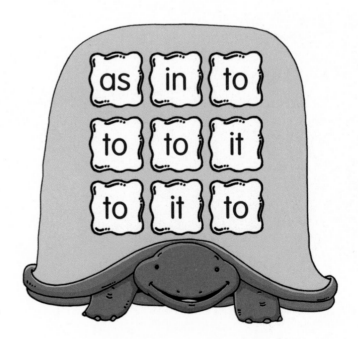

as	in	to
to	to	it
to	it	to

Trace it.

in   in   in

Write it.

Color the letters that spell in.

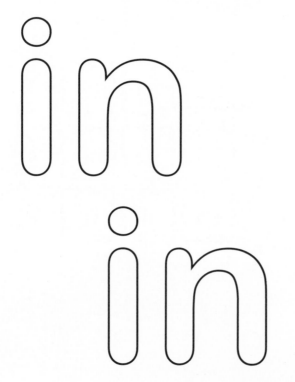

on

Trace it.

on   on   on

Write it.

Circle each bee with on.

on   an

in

on   on

Trace it.

Trace it.

it   it   it

Write it.

Write it.

Write it on each spaceship.

Circle each pair of glasses that spell as.

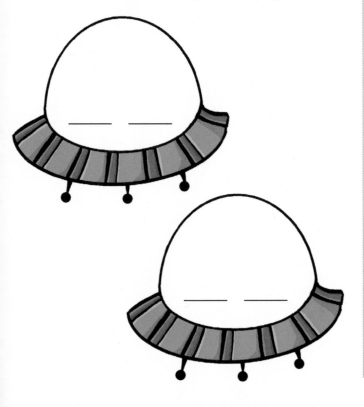

Build a word pyramid. Fill in the letters one at a time.
The first one is done for you.

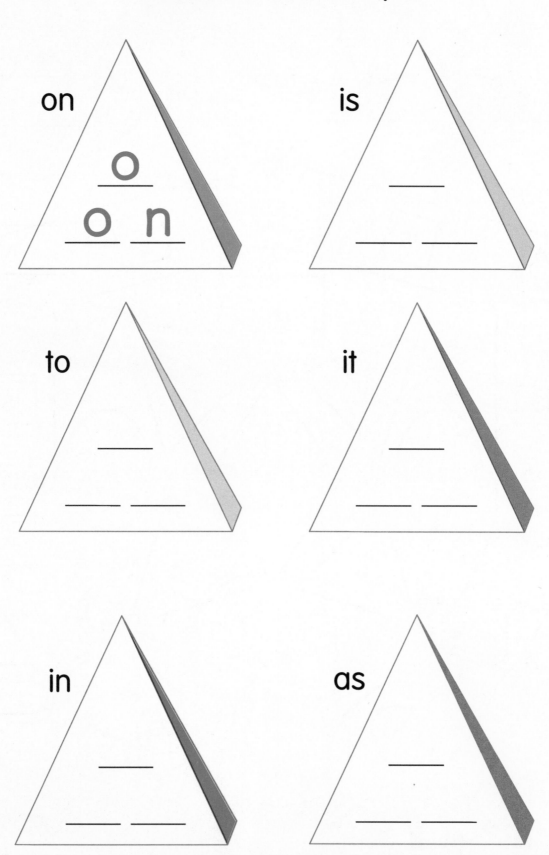

Color the picture. Use the color key.

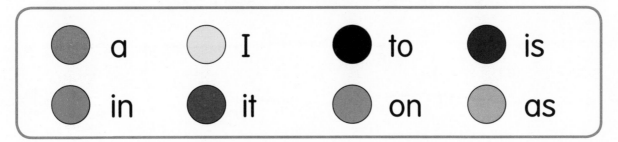

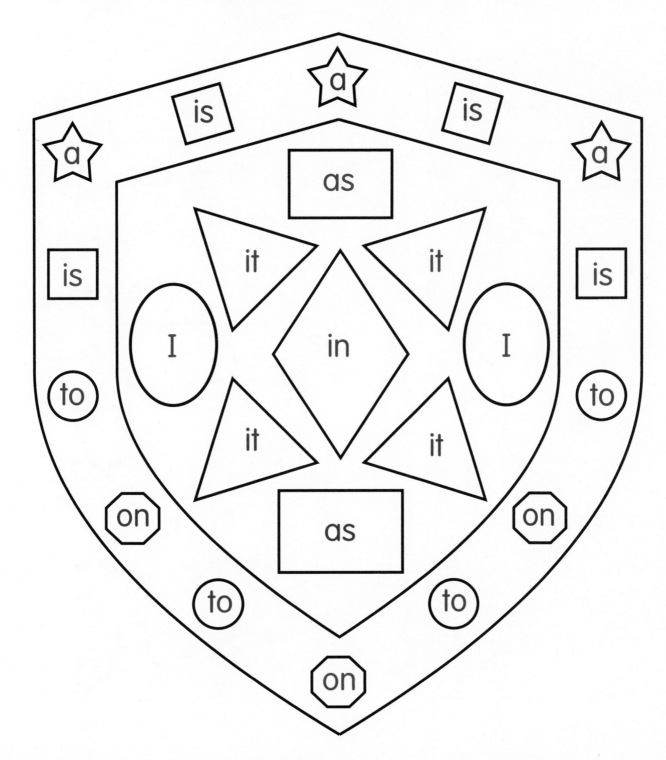

9

Unscramble each sight word.

as   in   to   it   is   on

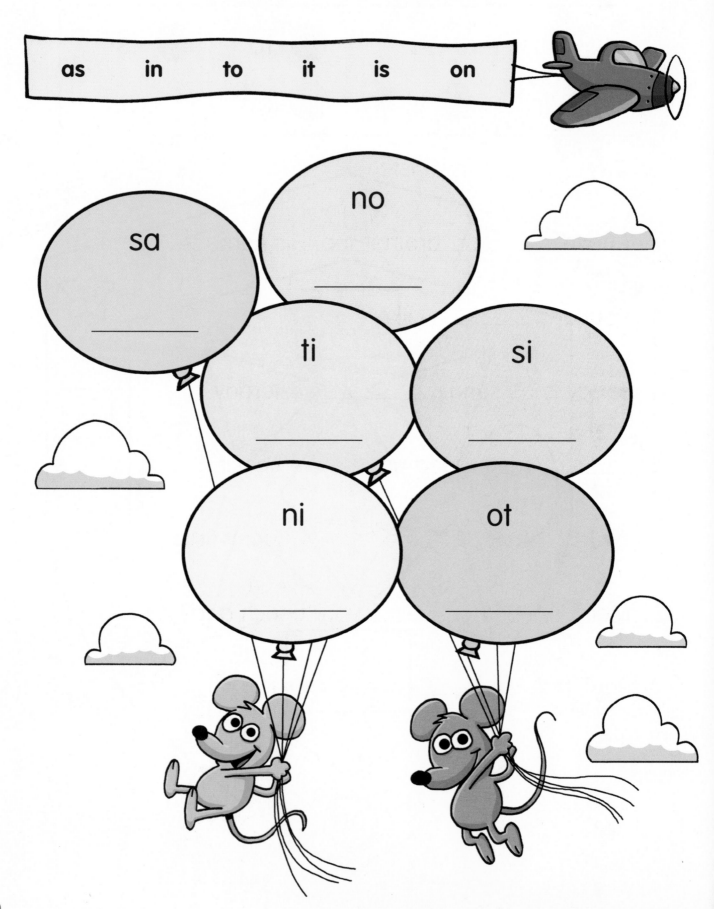

no
_____

sa
_____

ti
_____

si
_____

ni
_____

ot
_____

Choose a word from the list to complete the sentences.

Sight Words

a	as	I	in	is	it	on	to

REMEMBER TO capitalize the first word in a sentence.

1. This _____ my sister Molly.

2. I have _____ brother too. His name is Paul.

3. Paul and _____ like to swim.

4. Today is as sunny _____ yesterday.

5. _____ is a good day for the beach.

6. We go _____ the beach on sunny days.

7. Molly, what is _____ your beach bag?

8. Paul, put _____ your swim suit.

Trace it.

Trace it.

Write it.

Write it.

Color each space with at.

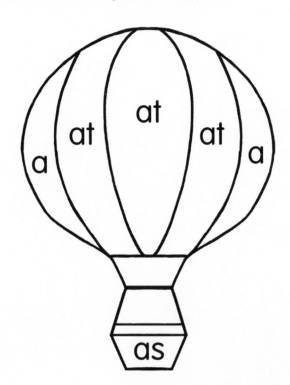

Circle each be.

Trace it.

or or or

Write it.

Write or on each bat.

_ _

_ _

Trace it.

an an an

Write it.

Trace the path that has an.

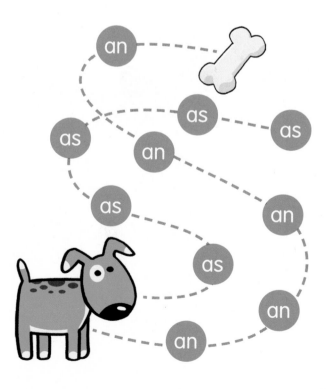

an as as
as an
as an
as an
an an

Trace it.

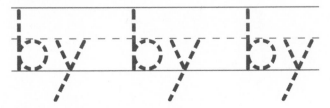

Write it.

_____

- - - - - - - - - - - - - - -

_____

Color the boxes that have by.

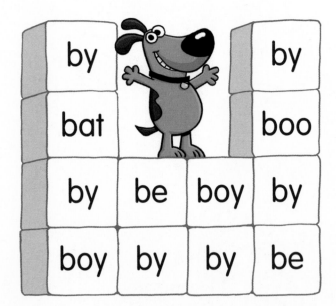

by		by
bat		boo
by	be	boy	by
boy	by	by	be

Trace it.

Write it.

_____

- - - - - - - - - - - - - - -

_____

Write he on each ball.

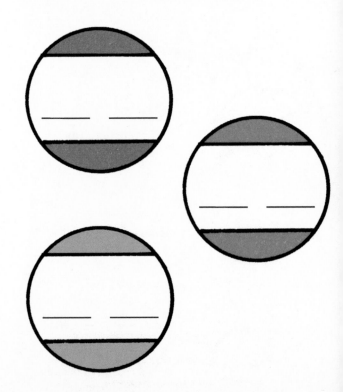

Trace it.

Trace it.

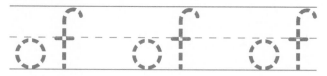

Write it.

Write it.

Color each hat that has we.

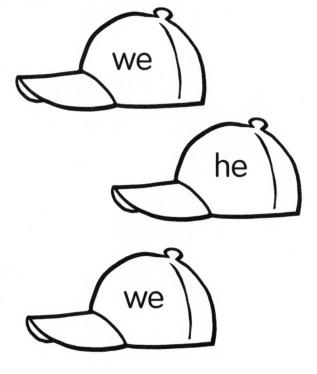

Circle each ice cream scoop that has of.

Build a word pyramid. Fill in the letters one at a time.
The first one is done for you.

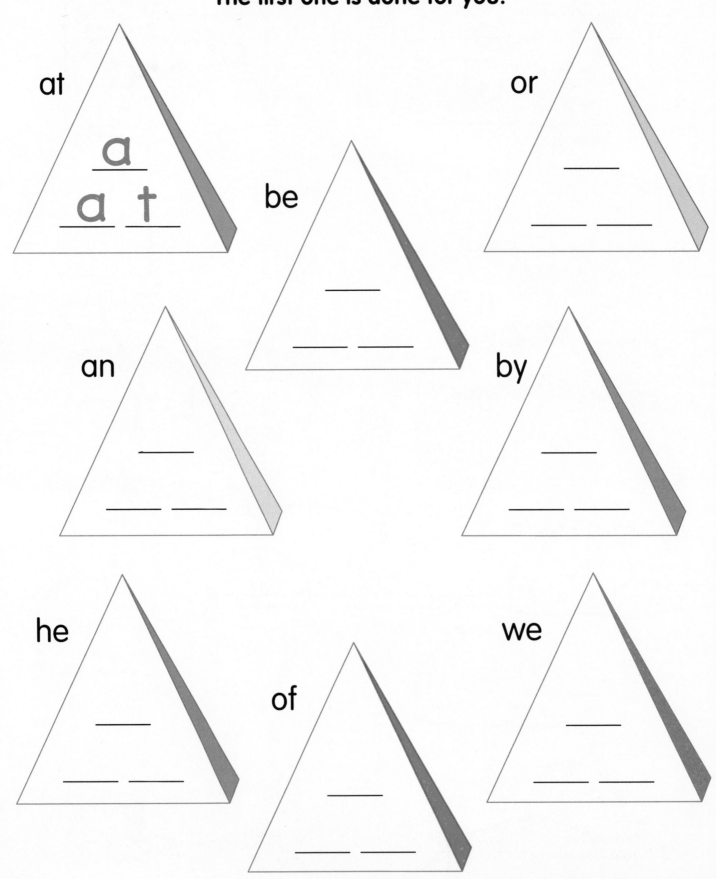

at

$\dfrac{a}{}$

$\dfrac{a}{}\ \dfrac{t}{}$

be

or

an

by

he

of

we

Color the picture. Use the color key.

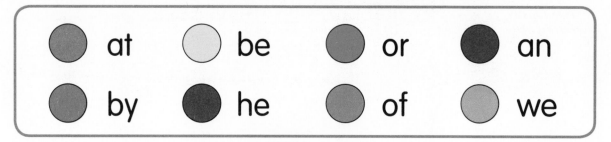

at   be   or   an
by   he   of   we

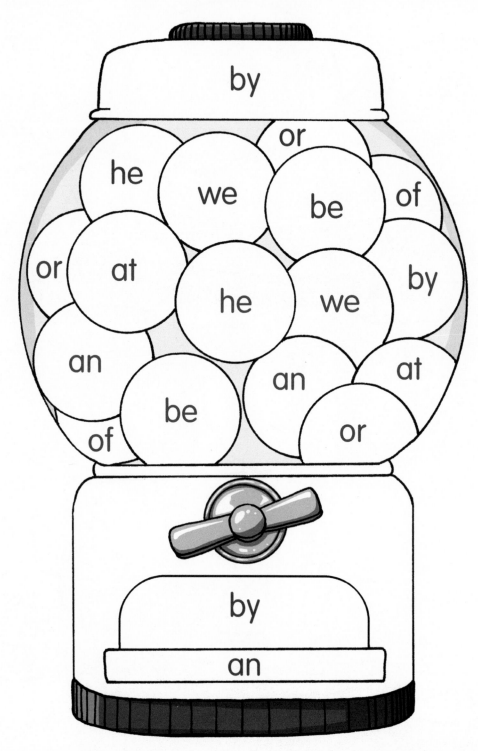

Unscramble each sight word.

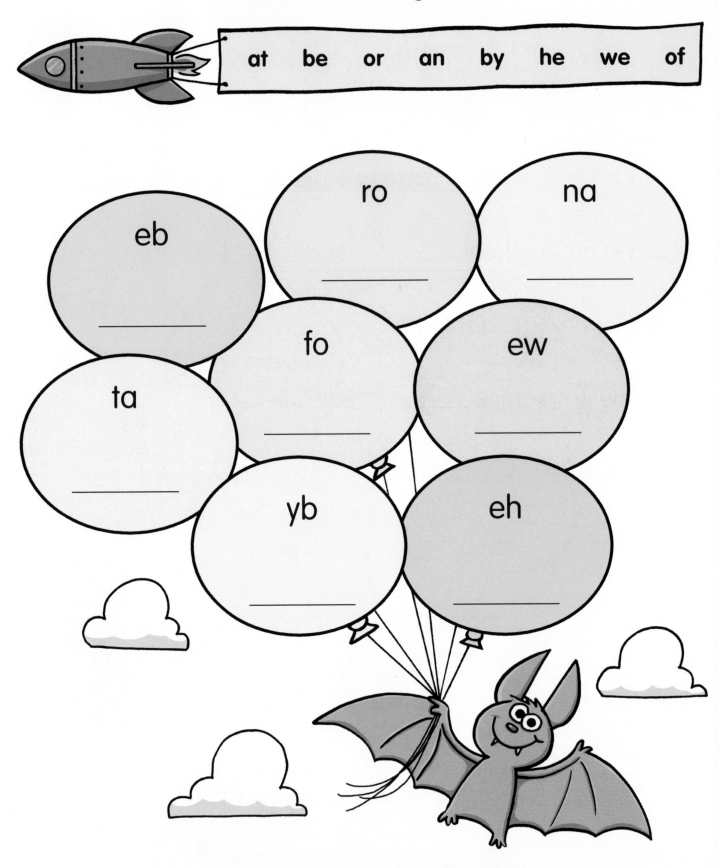

at   be   or   an   by   he   we   of

ro

na

eb

fo

ew

ta

yb

eh

Choose a word from the list to complete the sentences.

Sight Words

| an | at | be | by | he | of | or | we |

1. I have a twin brother. _____ are in the first grade.

2. We go to school _____ bus.

REMEMBER TO capitalize the first word in a sentence.

3. Mom always says, "Don't _____ late."

4. The bus comes _____ 8:00 A.M.

5. We must leave early _____ we will miss it.

6. This is a picture _____ George.

7. _____ is the school bus driver.

8. George does _____ important job.

all

and

Trace it.

all all all

Trace it.

and and

Write it.

Write it.

Color the letters that spell all.

all
all

Connect the dots to spell and.

•a

•n

•b

•d

•m

•p

Trace it.

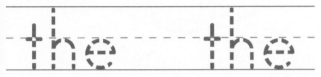

Write it.

Write the missing letters to spell the.

Trace it.

Write it.

Color each balloon that has are.

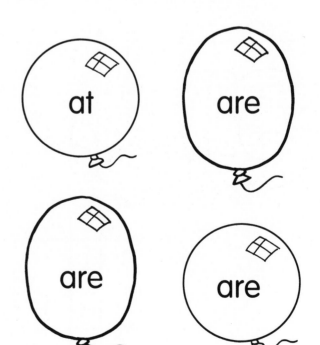

Trace it.

for for

Write it.

Write for on each bowl.

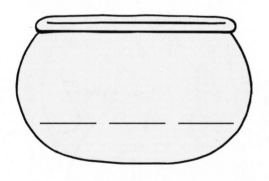

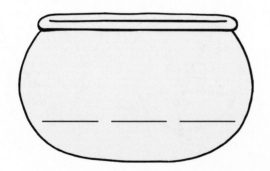

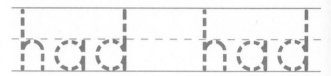

Trace it.

had had

Write it.

Trace the path that has had.

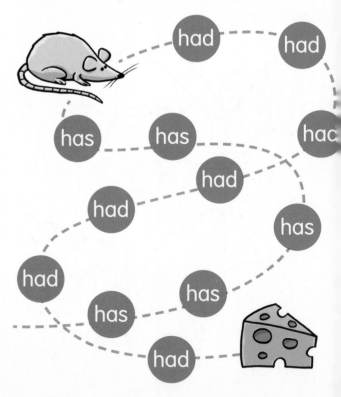

22

can

Trace it.

can   can

Write it.

Color each butterfly wing that has can.

can   can
call   call

cake   cake
can   can

but

Trace it.

but   but

Write it.

Circle each but.

but
but   bul
bat   bet
but

Build a word pyramid. Fill in the letters one at a time.
The first one is done for you.

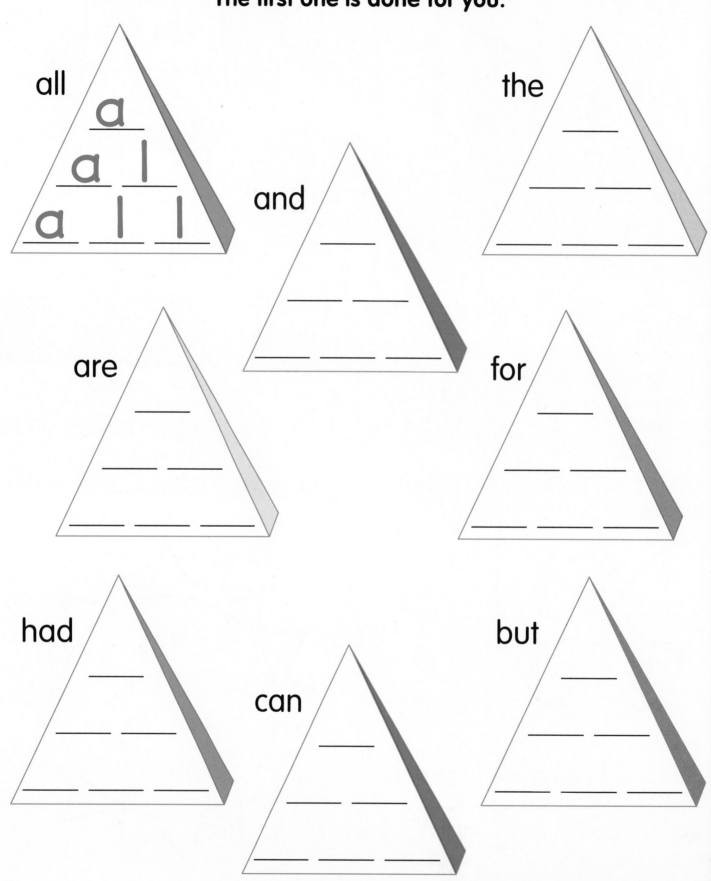

all

the

and

are

for

had

but

can

Color the picture. Use the color key.

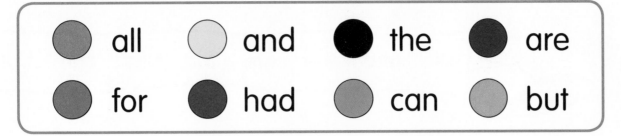

all   and   the   are

for   had   can   but

Unscramble each sight word.

all   and   the   are   for   had   can   but

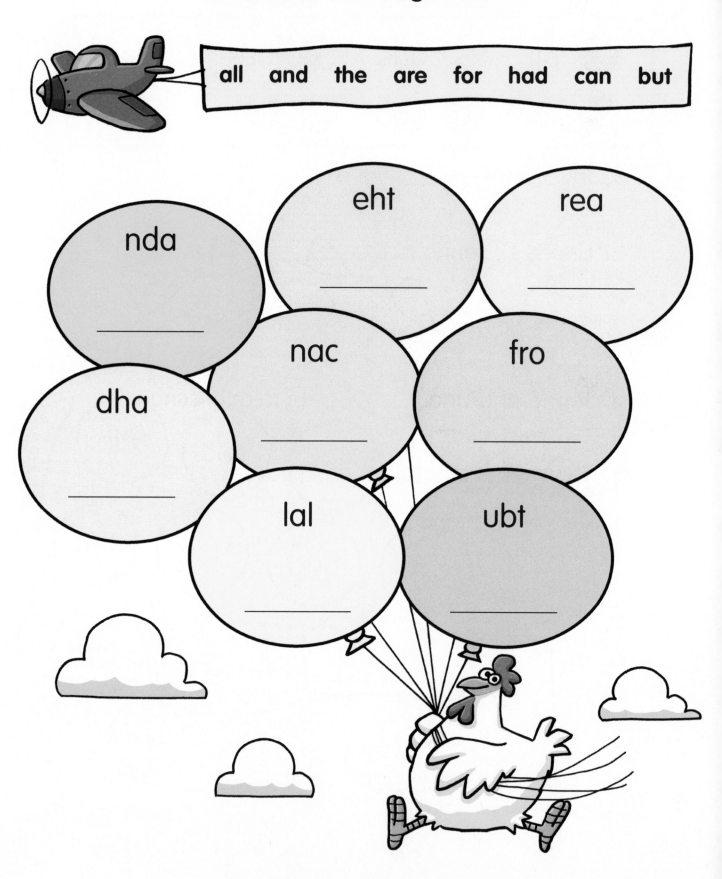

nda
_____

eht
_____

rea
_____

dha
_____

nac
_____

fro
_____

lal
_____

ubt
_____

Choose a word from the list to complete the sentences.

Sight Words

all	and	are	but	can	for	had	the

1. My sisters are _____ older.

2. Lina is 11, Jenna is 13, _____ Ria is 15.

3. Ria is older, _____ Jenna is taller.

4. Jenna and Lina _____ in middle school.

5. They take _____ bus to school.

6. Lina ran _____ class president.

7. She _____ the most votes.

8. I _____ be class president too one day.

Trace it.

you you

Write it.

Color each space with you.

you		you	
		one	two
yes	you	you	you
you	your	yet	out

not

Trace it.

not not

Write it.

Write not on each flag.

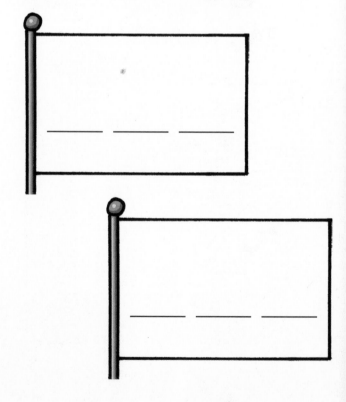

Trace it.

one one

Write it.

Circle each one.

one	now
an	one
one	won
ran	one

Trace it.

this this

Write it.

Color the two socks with the letters that spell this.

th   is   en

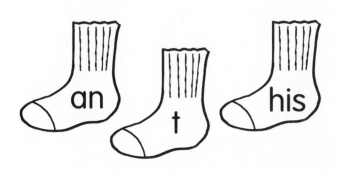

an   t   his

Trace it.

Trace it.

Write it.

Write it.

Write the missing letters to spell from.

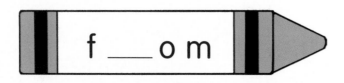

f __ o m

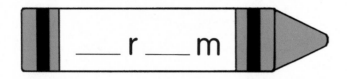

__ r __ m

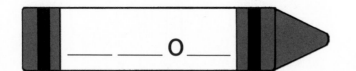

__ __ o __

Find the word with five times.

W	I	T	H	Z	A
I	Q	W	I	T	H
T	I	N	W	S	W
H	N	D	I	B	I
D	X	W	T	X	T
J	E	Z	H	H	H

they

Trace it.

they

Write it.

Circle each they.

they

thei

thay

they

they

they

thay

what

Trace it.

what

Write it.

Color each bone that has what.

what

when

where

what

Write each sight word in the shape box it fits.
The first one is done for you.

Sight Words

you	from
not	with
one	they
this	want

y o u

Color the picture. Use the color key.

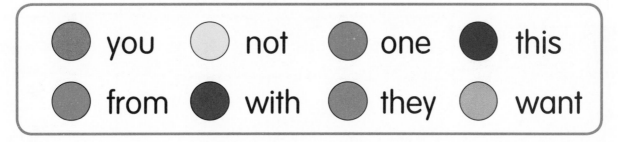

- ⬤ you
- ◯ not
- ⬤ one
- ⬤ this
- ⬤ from
- ⬤ with
- ⬤ they
- ⬤ want

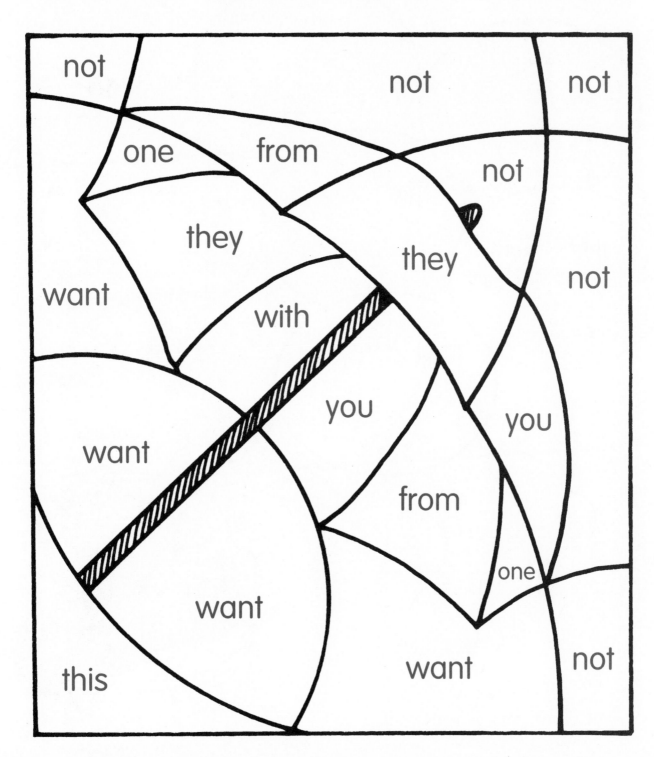

Unscramble each sight word.

you not one this from with they want

tsih

_____

ntwa

_____

heyt

_____

hwit

_____

eno

_____

oyu

_____

ont

_____

rfmo

_____

34

Choose a word from the list to complete the sentences.

Sight Words							
from	not	one	they	this	want	with	you

1. Maya's family is _____ Utah.

REMEMBER TO capitalize the first word in a sentence.

2. _____ moved here last year.

3. _____ is their house.

4. Maya's Grandma lives _____ them.

5. Maya is _____ of my best friends.

6. Maya and I _____ to travel.

7. We do _____ know where yet.

8. _____ can come too!

was

Trace it.

was   was

Write it.

Connect the dots to spell was.

•w

•a

•b

•c

•s

•m

•a

•n

she

Trace it.

she   she

Write it.

Write she.

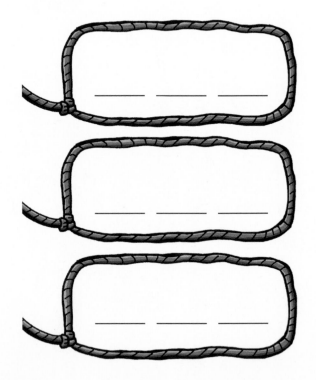

36

said

Trace it.

said

Write it.

Find the word said five times.

S	A	I	D	Z	A
I	Q	S	A	I	D
S	I	N	S	T	W
A	N	S	A	I	D
I	X	Y	I	A	T
D	E	Z	D	H	H

were

Trace it.

were

Write it.

Color each bubble that has were.

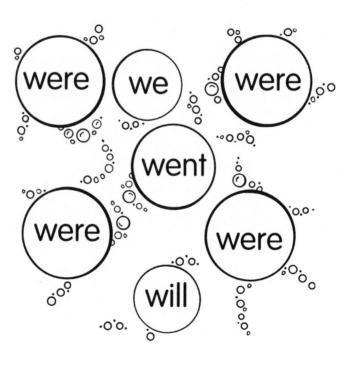

were   we   were

went

were   were

will

Trace it.

your

Write it.

Color each fish that has your.

your

you

pour

your

Trace it.

have

Write it.

Circle each have.

have

has

how

have

him

have

Trace it.

when

Write it.

Trace it.

that

Write it.

Color the letters that spell when.

when

when

Write the missing letters to spell that.

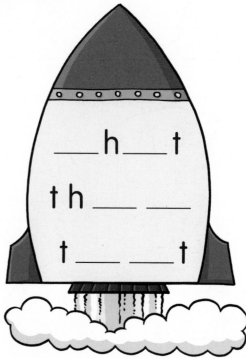

__ h __ t

t h __ __

t __ __ t

Write each sight word in the shape box it fits.
The first one is done for you.

Sight Words

was	have
said	were
she	when
that	your

w a s

Color the picture. Use the color key.

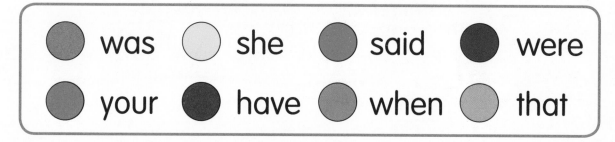

○ was ○ she ○ said ○ were
○ your ○ have ○ when ○ that

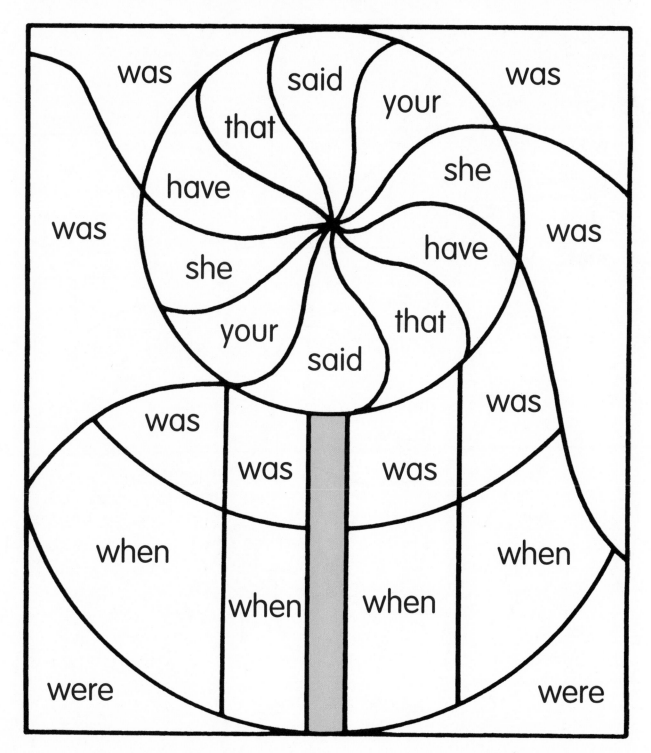

Unscramble each sight word.

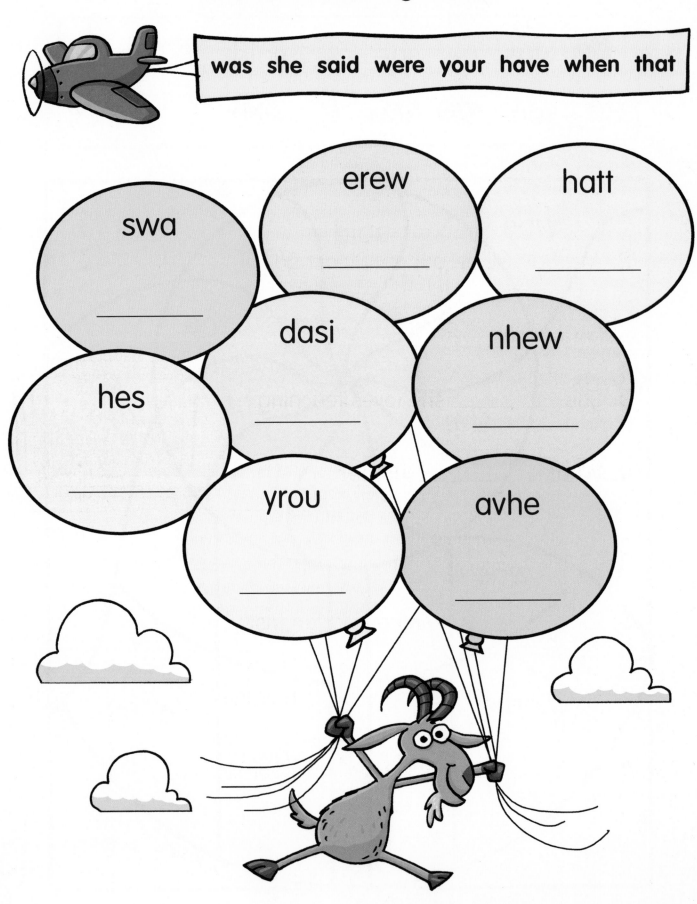

was   she   said   were   your   have   when   that

erew
_____

hatt
_____

swa
_____

dasi
_____

nhew
_____

hes
_____

yrou
_____

avhe
_____

42

Choose a word from the list to complete the sentences.

Sight Words

have   said   she   that   was   were   when   your

1. Yesterday _____ the first day of school.

2. Ms. Pat will be our new teacher.

   _____ teaches first grade.

REMEMBER TO capitalize the first word in a sentence.

3. She _____ she loves teaching.

4. What is _____ name?

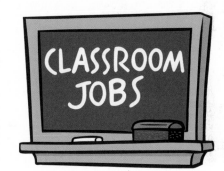

CLASSROOM JOBS

5. _____ did you start school?

6. _____ you in Kindergarten last year?

7. We will _____ a holiday party this year.

8. I know _____ you will love our class.

Draw lines from each end of the bridge to match the sight words.

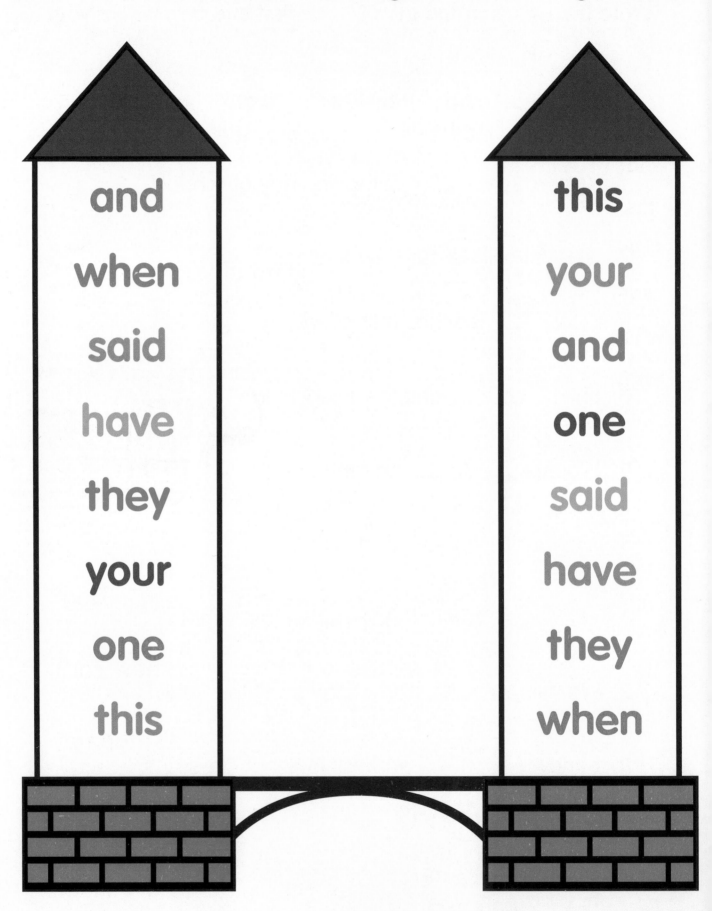

and
when
said
have
they
your
one
this

this
your
and
one
said
have
they
when

Complete the sentences. Choose a word from the list. Write the words in the puzzle. The first one is done for you.

Sight Words

that

the

they

was

what

with

Across

2. Where are ___they___ going?

3. I walk to school _____ friends.

4. He _____ at camp all summer.

REMEMBER TO capitalize the first word in a sentence.

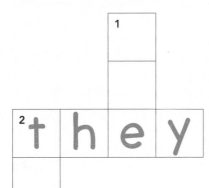

² t h e y

Down

1. Where is _____ dog?

2. Is _____ a new car?

3. _____ is your name?

45

Read each sentence. Match each sentence with a picture.

•   • **He** plays soccer.

•   • **All** the mice ate cheese.

•   • The cats **are** sleeping.

•   • They **were** playing with blocks.

•   • Mia eats **an** ice cream cone.

Write a sentence using at least one of the words in blue.

_____

_____

_____

Some words on the board are missing letters. Use the Letter Bank. Fill in the missing letters. The first one is done for you.

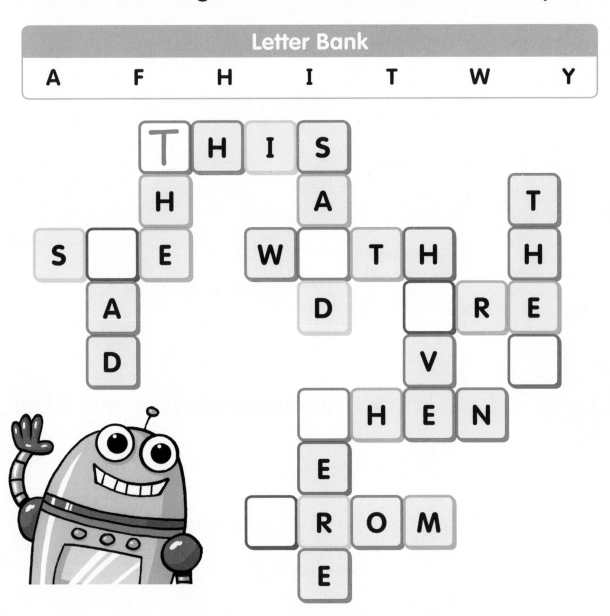

Letter Bank						
A	F	H	I	T	W	Y

Write the words from the game board on the lines.

THIS _____ _____ _____

THE _____ _____ _____

_____ _____ _____ _____

Answer Key

Page 11
1. is 2. a 3. I 4. as
5. It 6. to 7. in 8. on

Page 19
1. We 2. by 3. be
4. at 5. or 6. of
7. He 8. an

Page 27
1. all 2. and 3. but
4. are 5. the 6. for
7. had 8. can

Page 35
1. from 2. They 3. This
4. with 5. one 6. want
7. not 8. You

Page 43
1. was 2. She 3. said
4. your 5. When 6. Were
7. have 8. that

Page 45
Across: 2. they, 3. with, 4. was;
Down: 1. the, 2. that, 3. What

Page 47